COAL HARD
HABITAT

THE TRAVAILS OF A COAL MINER'S SON
PART ONE 1831-1848

JOANNE LEILA SMITH

Coal Hard Habitat is a poignant and introspective, three-part journal that charts the travails and triumphs of Will Gethyn's journey from boyhood to manhood, from ignominy to fame, from life to death. Based on both fictitious and real events and people who lived between the 1830s – 1840s in the UK to the 1850s to early 1900s in Australia, through Gethyn's life, we are invited to examine the human experience in our brightest and darkest hours.

Publisher Details

SOT Publications Co Pty Ltd
NSW, Australia

ISBN 978-0-9945367-2-3

SOT Publications Pty Ltd
PO Box 608
Woy Woy NSW 2256

Publisher's Cataloging-in-Publication data

Smith, Joanne Leila
Coal Hard Habitat: Part One 1831-1848. The Travails of a Coal Miner's
Son. / Writer Smith, Joanne Leila; with Illustrator Darlene Lavett.

Cover design and book layout by Briar Forrester.
Image of author by Sammer Affridi

ISBN 978-0-9945367-2-3

First Edition. Published in 2017.

Dedication
For the honour of my Maker, the God of Abraham.

Is not this earth our common also, as well as it is the common of brutes? May we not eat herbs, berries, or nuts as well as other creatures? Have we not a right to hunt and prowl for prey with she-wolves? And have we not a right to fish with she-otters? Or may we not dig coals or cut wood for fuel? Nay, does nature provide a luxuriant and abundant feast for all her numerous tribes of animals except us? As if sorrow were our portion alone, and as if we and our helpless babes came into this world only to weep over each other? (Thomas Spence 1797)

CHAPTER ONE

My Dad used to say that nothing felt as desolate as standing outside an abandoned mine. I am a coal miner's son. As is my father, and his father before. My father also told me that to God belongs all that is under the earth and on the earth and above it and not to let any lawman convince me otherwise. What lies beneath these soft green valleys feed our families, and it is the pride of a man to do so.

My mother died, giving birth to her first son in 1831, in a coal miner's cottage by the Swansea Docks in the South Wales Valleys. And as I write this, so many years later, on the other side of the world, I realise the picture in my mind of walking through Penllergare Woods to the mine with my father is dim, but the sense, the memory, the smells of grass dew mingled with cold black earth is vivid, without pause.

My father told me that the year I was born, Dic Penderyn – a stand up man, so my Dad said - was framed for killing a soldier as comeuppance for his hand in the Merthyr Rising to get better conditions for us miners. When he stood at the gallows, he said, "O Lord, here is iniquity". He was only 23 when the judge snapped his neck. All men, rich or poor, have the violent urge, the fear of poverty that claws at your guts and many men give their will to it. Whether you're wearing fine linen breeches or running bare, where there's money to be made, iniquity runs like an unbridled mare in heat.

The South Wales Valleys! Men have been looking up her skirts and shaking her upside down to give up her gold, her slate, her fine metals, her thick black coal since the Romans humbled her under their iron fist.

The Valleys stretch from eastern Carmarthenshire to western Monmouthshire and from the Heads of the Valleys in the north to the lower lying pastures of the Vale of Glamorgan and the coastal plain around Swansea Bay, Bridgend, Cardiff and Newport. Just as the valleys sit parallel to each other, so too were the daily lives of men who entered the mine just before sunrise and walked out of its dark mouth into the spreading darkness over the hills in evening. Shades of dark was the light of the coal miner. There were however, three glorious weeks in the heart of the summer months when a miner delighted in coming out of the pit to breath in fresh air warmed by the late afternoon sun – as if she was some golden haired angel, running late for tea, waiting to pop a kiss on your cheek before she took off over the hill again.

The Pit my Dad and me worked at was a drift mine, that is, it's an incline entry into the side of the hill face, which evens out once you get to the coal seam. By the time I was thirteen, there must have been over a hundred drift mines and nearly thirty shaft mines in the Valleys. Our Pit produced steam coal. It burns long and hot with little ash. The shinier the coal the better it was. Like most things in life I guess. Coal powered steam engines that drove steamships, locomotives and dreadnoughts of her majesty's fleet. Dad said that just as a man's flesh is renewed by the blood that flows through our veins, so the coal seam is the vein that keeps civilisation moving forward. My Dad was rarely wrong on things that mattered.

Anyway, being a coal miner was a tough lot, but we was tough men, 64 blokes in a row, coaxing a coal seam with a Cornish pickaxe and shovel. We foraged alongside rats. Laying on our sides, standing and hunched over. Burrowing, tunneling, digging and loading our black prize onto horse and gin cart. Sometimes, the seam wouldn't give too easy, so we'd blast it with dynamite to make her more amenable.

My name is Will Gethyn. I started working the mine when I was eight years old. At first us kids would hang around the top of the pit, helping to sort the coal from rock until you could prove that you weren't no trouble and could follow instructions without asking twice. Once you had established a wit about you, you'd get the nod to pick up an axe and show you could hold your own counsel just as good as any other bloke. The kids who had nouse but not enough strength to swing an axe, mostly petticoats, could go down into the pit too. They worked as Putters; dragging a cart of coal on all fours, strapped up with a belt and chain along the mine tunnel. If you was small, you was a Trapper. These kids opened and shut the timber doors to direct air through tunnels. That was a dead boring job and I was glad that the Lord made me broader than most boys my age.

Sarah, she was the same age as me and we was best mates. I was going to marry her one day. As soon as she'd let me kiss her, I was going to ask her to be mine. Sarah was a Trapper. She reckons when I'm scrubbed up in my Sunday best, my hair is the colour of a dull brass bell and my eyes the colour of molasses. I think Sarah is the most beautiful girl the Valley ever did yield, with her strawberry curls and deep green eyes.

By the time I was thirteen, the Deputy gave me a pick and shovel. Of course, it wasn't free, it was deducted from my wage, which was two crowns a week. I worked in a different crew from my Dad, even though

"Dad said that just as a man's flesh is renewed by the blood that flows
through our veins, so the coal seam is the vein that keeps civilisation
moving forward. My Dad was rarely wrong on things that mattered."

we worked the same seam, he being deeper into the tunnel and I worked in the crew near the tunnel opening. I didn't see him during the day, so the morning and evening walks home was when I dragged my feet, asking about everything and anything cause once we got home, Dad wasn't much for talking.

Now most young blokes, when they get a hold of an axe, they are all eager like, making out tough by swinging hard from end to end. My Dad said showing off is a tiring pursuit, and most young fellas give too much power from the start of the swing. The old blokes know that you gotta start soft on the swing, and once it reaches straight over your head, you accelerate down with power – it helps you keep your energy for longer and the force of your strike harder.

There was no machines at a miner's disposal in them days. Industry relied on the backs of hard men, grappling in the dark for an easy cleat to drive their wedge and break the ribs of the coal face. Three tonnes of coal was the daily output of one man's will and brute force. And it just so happens that three tonnes of coal produced one tonne of iron.

Most of the mining folk got on well enough. Like I said before, we all wore the same cut of collar, so we mostly looked out for each other. As human nature would have it, there was always blokes trying to find some way to one up themselves, so they'd imagine a divide between religion or race and cause trouble in the village. They'd let out their hate in the boxing ring, as sport was the only arena they could pretend they didn't have to rely on each other. Dad made me promise to steer clear from men of that disposition and to this day, I hope I stayed true to my word...Now look at that, I'm getting ahead of myself. I sometimes have an inclination to do that, when I feel like I have a story to tell. It might be best to start from the beginning, from the day when my life changed forever...

CHAPTER TWO

"Percy you fat bastard!" said Gethyn as he friendly slapped the Hoister on his back.

The sun had just touched the peak of the hill in the east as Dad and me arrived at the Pit. Percy liked his lunch, and rumour had it, he liked other miners' lunches too. Of course, you couldn't go 'round making accusations. Anyone caught prigging another man's lunch would get beaten with a stick, and besides, even if Percy was helping himself to someone's grub, Dad said Percy was too shifty to get nailed. Put me off me lunch thinking of Percy's five fat fingers foraging round for food.

"Lucky for yer pit rats Gethyn, not being able to see yer ugly mug. Get in the Dolly then, enough friskin' make it snappy lads," said Percy as he rang the bell three times, which was signal code for men coming down into the pit.

Dad climbed in after me and closed the Dolly Cart side door. We sat at the opening of the shaft as Percy cranked the release cable and we slowly moved down into the dark tunnel. It's a strange feeling, with your back to the mine, watching the blue light outside seem close but getting far away. Three quarter ways down, the air sharply turns a deep black cold and sound is immediate when the light is gone.

Us miners see with our ears. We know more of what's going on 'round us by listening real close like. The coal in the seam makes a pressing sound when you hit it. Water trickles down the fissures in the roof and the ribs of the coalface. Too much shale in the strata creates downward pressure and makes a cracking noise.

We test a competent roof with our ears too. Dad says 'that it's a good roof that's gonna squash ya 'cause you can spot a saggin' roof from a mile away'. That's the trick about a good roof, it makes you complacent. Dad says to think of a roof like a petticoat. She's inconsistent. One day she says we're solid, and the next day she's had a change of heart. The roof gets a fracture, which turns into a series of fractures and then the roof is no longer reliable... So that's why you need to sound the roof first. If you hit it with the end of your axe and if it makes a solid ringing noise, you got yourself a competent roof, but a dull thud means it's a roof with lots of cracks in it. Either way, it'll all cave in eventually and time changes everything.

When we arrived at the mustering point in the Pit, a few of the miners were standing around hobnobbin' the Deputy, huddled like, which is fairly odd as the Deputy likes to bark when giving orders. It is an eerie thing, watching black shapes jump along the walls from the candle lights on our caps. Dad told me to go straight to my crew as he walked over towards the Deputy to see what the fuss was about.

There was eight men working one panel in every crew, and we was currently working eight panels per crew. Our pit was a room and pillar extraction, which means we take about half the coal and leave the other in place to support the roof, like pillars, and the room is an empty gob after taking out the coal.

We undermine from the bottom of the rib first and then the top to help break the coal easy, as the top of the wall would lose support from underneath and be easier to break through.

Our dag is ten skips a day so we try to load the coal fast onto the skip and pony. Jimmy, he's the guy in our crew who puts the props and crib in to prevent the roof from caving in once the coal is taken away. The props are only on one side to get the skip through.

I asked my Dad once how far do you know how to extract? Dad said, 'that if a man is squashed diggin' two yards in, then you reduce the next dig to one and a half. Experience is written in blood'.

Dad said to listen for props cracking while we're working a room 'cause it's an early sign of weight pushin' down. The more the cracking increases in rate, the props bend and break in succession, like how thunder rolls in as the lightening gets closer.

"Mornin' Will," said Sharpy as I took my first swing in the line on our panel.

"Hey Sharpy."

"Where's yer old man? Haven't seen him this mornin'"

"Yeah. He's yabbin' with the Deputy. What's goin' on yer know?"

"Hess ain't got a good draft in at the furnace. There's been no wind for over a week."

"There's plenty of wind comin' from Aaron's corner," said Sharpy.

That's 'cause I've been breakin bread at yer missus table," said Aaron.

Will smiled as he felt along the ribs with his fingers for an easy cleat to drive his wedge in. There's no echo underground, just a dull sound as if you're in a huge damper. He lifted up his axe and kept swinging in tight with Aaron and Sharpy.

"Here comes yer petticoat for her mornin' tickle," teased Aaron.

"Stow yer mag," said Will quietly. His heart jumped.

"Dad says to think of a roof like a petticoat. She's inconsistent. One day she says we're solid, and the next day she's had a change of heart."

"Hi Will," Sarah stood to the side out of the axe's path.

Will kept his swing on without pause. He wanted to look at Sarah real bad, but he didn't want to lose face in front of the other guys.

"I'll chat up top later," grunted Will, not turning around.

"Suit yerself," Sarah shrugged and kept walking.

In some parts of the mine, it was very damp and wet up to your knees in other parts, sludgy black silt. The water runs clear before you trample through it 'cause it's spring mountain water. Will liked being in this part of the mine as it was fairly dry with fine coal dust and, when he looked up at the low black roof the light from the candles made the small beads of condensation look like shining stars in a moonless sky.

The men fell into quiet unison for the next hour while they chipped away at the coal face as the fellas behind shoveled the coal into piles and on the skips. Once you get into a rhythm, time passes in a hypnotic way when there's no natural light.

"Hey, did ya hear 'bout that suckhole Smivvy on Sat'dy night? What a disgrace," said Aaron breaking the reverie.

"No," said Will.

"Wasn't talkin to yer boy," said Aaron.

Will held his peace. He wasn't fond of Aaron. One day he's friendly like and the next he acts as if you don't exist. Dad says Aaron's like his old man, a Skycer – He's mean most of the time and is only cordial if he wants something from ya.

Suddenly, Will heard a loud bang shudder from deep inside the tunnel.

"It's a bag of fuckin' foulness!" a voice hysterically shouted down the line as a series of popping cracks beared down like a screaming steam engine racing towards Will. His knuckles gripped the axe handle in panic and he felt his legs turn to lead as an unseen force picked him up and threw him up the line against the wall into a numbing drone that slowly turned into silent blackness.

Chapter Three

Will felt his sense slowly return to him. He flexed and stretched slightly, wincing from a broad ache right through his toes to temple. He tried to open his eyes but his lids felt so heavy, as if his eyelids were struggling to lift through black sticky tar. He opened his eyes and saw nothing and shut them. He drifted back into a dark dead sleep.

Outside, the sun and moon chased each other in a pale blue void before Will regained full consciousness again. He could feel himself crumpled on his side on the floor. He opened his eyes into soundless black. The full force of understanding his predicament gripped his throat and he let out a choked hoarse howl. The floor was a cold shoulder to his grief.

"Dad!" he cried out in distress. "Dad! Dad, Dad! Dad, Dad!"

"Sarah!! Sarah!!"

"Mam, Mammy! Mammy!" He put his hands over his brow and wept.

"Is anyone here?" Will cried and lifted himself off the floor. He felt his body carefully for open wounds and breaks and found none. The discovery of this was enough to calm his breathing into a steady rhythm.

Will recalled hearing someone yell a "bag of foulness," and he realised that must have been why the Deputy was worried about the lack of wind. Dad said once if there's not enough wind in the mine, gas builds up and can cause explosions. He told me that gas gathers in pockets, slowly cooking like a kettle on the flame in the coal and rock, and when you dig into it, the release of pressure can create a series of explosions. He also said he had heard that gas explosions can happen from sparks when coal was struck with the axe with too much coal dust in the air.

Will realised that if he was going to attempt to make it out of the mine, he would not be able to light his candle.

"Better croak tryin' than sittin' here like a whingin' minge," Will tough talked his tears off his face and set his soft mouth into a hard grimace.

He stood up and fumbled along the ribs of the wall to find the rope. In an underground pit, a rope was fixed with an arrow block timber every twenty metres. The side of the smaller point of the block indicated which way was out.

He felt the coarse cord at knee length and his heart jumped in hope. He gripped the line. Here we go, Will said to himself. He held the line between his hand, walking carefully for a few minutes until he hit a wall. Will dropped the cord in terror. Panicking, he felt along the width of the wall, the surface crumbling loosely in his hands. He let out a long wail as he realised what he was feeling was coal and rock that had collapsed due to the explosion.

"Dad! Dad! Don't leave me, don't leave me Dad, Dad!" Will wept.

He buried his face in the wall, with his arms outstretched hugging the loose coal as it crumbled around his feet. He fell to his knees and cried. He knew that if he started to dig into the wall, the roof may collapse further and he didn't know how far deep the collapse in the tunnel went. Will edged back to the rib of the coal face and fumbled for the cord. He paused, distraught. His heart squeezed tight as if he was climbing to heaven and he could feel his blood rushing through his body, as if it was trying to find a way to spurt out. He slowly turned his back to the wall and continued following the cord until he felt the timber arrow. He felt for the small point and was overcome with sick relief. Relieved that he had a life line, sick in not knowing if Dad and Sarah were on the other side of the collapsed wall. He lunged forward and immediately felt overcome with a nauseating dizziness and fell over. He hit his head on a rock and cried out.

He could feel the blood dripping into his eyes and wiped it away with the sleeve of his shirt. He sat for a few minutes before trying to stand, but the feeling of dizziness overcame him completely every time he tried. Walking upright in total blackness gave him vertigo. He stayed down, carefully crawling, like a black shadow crouching in candlelight, the hard edges of the bituminous coal scrapping his knees and hands whenever he lost balance and fell.

He paused after passing 11 timber blocks, calculating he had moved 220 yards from the collapsed wall.

The journey out was slow going and the terror of the roof collapsing was enough to keep Will crawling along until he could reach the mustering point. When Will's hand hit an obstacle, he let go of the line and felt around the object. It was a narrow table with a large wooden barrel of water on top. Will let out a shout of relief as he fumbled for the handle on the spigot. He turned it quickly and put his mouth over the end of the tap and drank the cold clean water and gasped. He washed his face, gingerly patting the temple where he had hit his head.

He knew he was very close to the mustering point now, it was just around the second bend of the main tunnel. Renewed with hope, he edged past the table and held the line, slowly crawling forward to the mustering point. The thought of seeing the light at the end of the tunnel and not being able to run towards it was nearly more than he could bear. After Will finally crawled past the first bend, the line stopped. Will had hit another wall. He fell back on his haunches in shock. The roof had collapsed. Will opened his mouth in horror but no sound came out.

At the shock of being caged in on both sides in the pit, Will crawled back to the table and moved any lumps of coal underneath so he could lay under it. Exhausted, he gingerly raised his hand and touched underneath the water table before putting his arm over his brow. He laid still in the black soundless void wondering how long it would take for him to die. Would I know when I was going to die and will it hurt? Dad said we were all born to die and I had given it no consideration. I am young, what is it my business to die? Death is the occupation of the old man or the mother in labour. What do I know of death when I know little of life? Will felt like a wild wolf was trapped inside his heart, scratching at the walls, tearing at his flesh inside out.

His Dad once told him that explosives have little power out in open spaces. They only make an impact if you pack the explosive in a confined space, with no entry, no exit. Trapped in the depths of the black earth, Will discovered his helplessness and his strength.

He felt a peculiar emptiness envelope him. He realised that there was no refuge from the darkness except in God. Will's soul cried out in its deepest distress, "God of Abraham! God of my salvation! Whatever good you got for me, I need it now Lord!" Will pulled his legs into his chest and wept bitterly.

CHAPTER FOUR

A subtle breeze passed over Will's face and he thought he must have been dreaming. Dad's awake, thought Will. He stirred, expecting to see the end of his iron bed. He opened his eyes and saw nothing. Will groaned and closed his eyes. He felt a faint draft pass over his face again. This time, the draft was like a shock of cold water being thrown on his face. Will sat very still and waited for the draft again. There! There it is! Will said to himself. Will opened his eyes.

"The ventilation shaft!" croaked Will, overcome with emotion.

Will crawled out from under the table and fumbled for another drink of water. He felt weak in his knees but his mind felt alert, sharp at the prospect of avoiding a lonely death.

The Swansea Pit had fire driven mine ventilation to prevent buildup of dangerous gases. Two vertical shafts were sunk, parallel, with the furnace and chimney stack between the two shafts above ground. The shaft to the left of the furnace, had a narrow tunnel halfway up the first shaft, which led, diagonally, into the furnace room. Here, each morning Hessy would light the fire, which would suck up the mine's air and gas mixture through the first shaft and draw out the gases through the chimney stack. The stale air would be replaced by fresh air drawn down into the second shaft to the right.

Will considered his predicament. If he was going to get to the fire shaft he would have to leave the life line in the main tunnel, find the goaf where the ventilation shafts were and try to crawl up into the furnace room through the narrow joining tunnel. I'll be guided by the draft, Will thought. Or do I stay here? I could get lost forever in one of them gobs and they'll never find me if they come looking for me. What do I do? Will closed his eyes and clenched his fists.

"Plummy. Let's get on with it then," said Will.

He crouched in the dark, like a tom cat, sensing with his ears and skin. He felt a draft coming from his right. He turned his back to the life line and crawled towards the draft, each time pausing for validation, before moving again toward the subtle wind. In absolute blackness, time is not measured. Will crawled and turned, to the left, to the right, to the right again. He didn't know how much time had passed or whether he was going in circles. All he knew was the coal under his hands and knees

"Would I know when I was going to die and will it hurt? Dad said we were all born to die and I had given it no consideration."

and the soft wind touching his face. As the draft felt more pronounced, Will pushed on towards it.

The closer he came towards the shaft, Will noticed the darkness lifted in slight degrees. Will's heart jumped in hope and pressed on towards the lightening blackness. When he finally reached the goaf, Will saw two white orbs of light at the base of the ventilation shafts.

The draft was very strong, as if the wind was cheering on Will to follow it up the shaft like a dandelion dispersing in a hot summer wind. Will's eyes welled in warm tears, and he half stood, half crawled to the light under the first shaft. He laid underneath it, the light shining on his face. His eyes blinked, adjusting to the light. Tears of gratitude streamed down his ashen face, white rivulets tracked down his cheeks and pooled in his ears. Thank you God, he whispered in his heart. He could see from the colour of the sky that the sun had just set.

"Hello! Anyone there!" Will yelled into the shaft.

No one answered.

Will stood up inside the base of the shaft and felt the walls of the rock. The seams ran horizontal and vertical. He knew he had thirty minutes of twilight until he was in darkness again. He extended his arm as far as he could until he found a handhold. Gripping it with his fingers he hoisted himself up with both legs and arms outspread against the sides of the walls.

Carefully he inched upward as fast as he could find hand and foot holds in the wall. Sections of the wall vary in strength and Will knew he only had to put too much weight on one side and he risked the handhold breaking. Don't give up! Will shouted in his head, salty sweat poured into his eyes. Don't give up, don't give up he kept on until he could see the narrow tunnel entry halfway up the shaft. He pressed upward, like a spider crawling up a glass tube.

"Nearly, Will, don't fall, keep going," he said to himself.

As he reached the opening of the diagonal tunnel, Will paused. He knew he only had one chance to let go of the other side of the wall and lunge his body forward far enough to give enough leverage to pull himself into the tunnel with both arms. Drawing on a deep breath through his nostrils, Will yelled as he let go and flung himself into the tunnel. He crawled like an earthworm, blindly pressing forward until he emerged at the base of the furnace room. Gripping the iron floor grill between both hands, he used the last of his strength to push it through. It fell with a loud clang.

Exhausted, Will pulled himself up out of the tunnel and passed out on the brick floor.

CHAPTER FIVE

Two sugar lumps clinked in a china cup. Steam from poured strong black tea interrupted by a teaspoon whirlpool. Lowered eyes, sympathetic tilts of the head, tight smiles, and furtive, curious glances in my general direction. Passing impressions was all I remembered of my father's funeral.

It is a strange thing to be standing at an empty grave. People giving reverence to a hole in the ground, as if my Dad could hear beneath the coal rubble below, a few miles away.

I was the sole survivor of what came to be known as the Swansea Pit Disaster of 1844.

At the reading of my father's Will, I found out I had an Aunt Betrys in London. The Minister said as my Aunt was my sole surviving next-of-kin (she was my mother's sister) therefore it being most appropriate, I was to leave for London as soon as I was able.

The Minister conferred with my neighbour, Mrs Abbott, - 'a meddlesome old bird' as Dad used to say – and they agreed to take care of the few belongings we had. So it was settled, and I was in no state to protest even if I felt contrary-wise. I had a strange numbness in spirit and my mind hadn't caught up at the notion of my new orphaned status.

Mrs Parkes from the company store, gave me a travel bag to pack my few belongings in, and the mining boss gave me five pounds for my loss and a stern handshake declaring the parting of our ways.

Dad and I had no savings, our livelihood combined paid our lodgings, meals, soap, gas and water. What little left over was for a small luxury – cured meat, a slab of sharpie cheese, a bottle of gin – when the occasion warranted.

I didn't go to Sarah's funeral. To tell it straight, I couldn't face her death. I had a guilty relief at not receiving an invitation. The thought of her broken in the dark… It was a place I never wanted to go back to so I kept her in my memory alive and well, laughing eyes bright and teasing.

So there I was. A coal miner's son without a father or a Mine to earn my provision. I didn't say nothing to anyone in case they could hear the upset in my voice, so I left early morning, with my possessions and the thought that the only thing I knew about my future was the itinerary of my departure and the address of Aunt Betrys in St Giles, London.

I handed my ticket to the Captain of a three-man crew, alighting at Swansea Canal to River Severn, disembarking at Gloucestershire Canal to catch my first train ride on the Great Western Railway at Gloucester directly to Euston Station, London.

I can't say I remember much about the journey along the canals, my mind being occupied with grief and my hands wrung sore. The train trip, however, I remember well. The locomotive was a roaring brown and cream beast that shook like a frenzied bull whether we be on an incline or going straight. I didn't know it at the time, but I was in a second class carriage, with benches holding five men abreast, face-to-face, chewing backey and every now and then, a snuff here, a puff there. The air was thick and astringent, reluctant to escape through a narrow window of timber louvers on the carriage doors.

Now, I can tell you square, there was nothing that could have prepared me for the shock of humanity when the carriage doors opened at Euston Station.

Before I could gather my bearings, I was knocked senseless by the smell of the place. I mean, there was dolled up Molls and Culls all going about their business, rushing to and fro on the concourse, walking around as if their noses took no offence. Fair play, the city smelt like a cross between a shitter and a dead rabbit stewing in the sun. I learnt to get used to it after a while, some days were harder than others though. The concourse was wide and grand, with a pitched iron roof and soaring arches held firm by proud columns standing in a row. There was bibles chained to stands for waiting passengers to read, and a queue a mile long at the booking office.

I walked out of the Station and stood on the side of the road, unsure of myself. It was early morning outside, but I couldn't see much in front of me in any direction. There was a hazy coal-smoke fog veiling a riot of sounds fighting for supremacy in the streets. There was scratching and screeching of wheels and galumphing of hooves on the pavement from coaches, cries from street kids and old folk selling all sorts of wares and scran to passengers going in and out of the main entry. Wagons and bells, dogs barking and workmen in all sorts of livery, some simple, some in fine silks with buffed brass buttons and buckled shoes, striped waist coats and fancy linen cuffs scuffling and parading along. I ain't never seen such finery.

There was a cab-stand with two watermen tending to the horses and washing down omnibuses with buckets, a sight I'd never known. They had seats inside and box seats up top next to the coachman.

Curious, I made my way towards the cab-stand, trying not to walk

"I can't say I remember much about the journey along the canals, my mind being occupied with grief and my hands wrung sore. The train trip, however, I remember well. The locomotive was a roaring brown and cream beast that shook like a frenzied bull whether we be on an incline or going straight."

in the muck on the edges the road, where the crossing sweeper boys swept the dung, mud and licky mac into piles, and careful not to get too close to the middle road, as there was no separation between footpath and carriageway. It was a slippery jig between falling in the muck or falling foul under a set of hooves. I learnt that there was an understood courtesy between cart and cull; when a coachman approached from behind a pedestrian, he'd yell "Heih! Heih!' to give you just enough time to step aside before they rattled past, his whip slicing air, His white top hat hanging on and a cheerful rose in his buttonhole.

"Mornin' Sir," said Will as he stood next to the dark brown bus.

"Leavin' in five," said the Coachman, without looking down. He had a giant black moustache that twirled into fine pointed peaks at each end.

"How much for a ride Sir?"

The Coachman looked down at Will, fingering his moustache. "You a Youkell then boy?"

"What's a Youkell Sir?"

"Either a countryboy or a clown, dependin' on me mood."

"I'm a coal miner Sir. How fast does she go?" Will nodded to the bus.

The Coachman shrugged. "It's 6d for a ride, but if it is speed you want Youkell, I'd suggest the mailcoach, they'll clock up a steady 14 miles an hour. Flag down a bright red undercarriage with Her Majesty's arms on the door, they always got room for a few extra deliveries. Cost yer 10d per mile though and by the looks of ya, yer ain't no squire rushin' to Dividend Day."

"Yes Sir. I need to get to St Giles," said Will.

"Ain't nobody needs to get to St Giles boy."

"What do you mean Sir?"

"You'd be better off walkin' if yer lodgings St Giles. Save yer tin."

"How do I get there? It's me first day here."

The Coachman stretched his hand out as he spoke. "The city follows the River on an east-west axis, with three main routes - Pall Mall via the Strand and Fleet Street to St Pauls; Oxford Street along High Holborn and the New Road. No road runs straight in this city boy, so bear yourself by the river and you'll find yer way. Walk down the end of this street, turn South, cross over New Road onto Tottenham Court, through Bloomsbury.

Once you hit Oxford Street, St Martin's or Drury Lanes will find yer at Seven Dials, St Giles. God's speed boy."

"Thank you," said Will.

"Don't want yer gratitude. Yer can flip me 3d, cause my advice saved yer another yer 3d."

Will felt for the money in his inside coat pocket and handed it to the Coachman.

Will tipped the top of his brown cap to the Coachman, and stepped back to allow for the passengers to scramble for the best seats up top. The coachman offered a short chap the end of his leather strap to help hoist himself onto the Driver's footboard and mount into the box seat next to the Driver. There was no decent way a petticoat could climb up top, Will thought. He peered inside the carriage. It was low-roofed and narrow, with filthy straw on the floor and two benches running parallel. He adjusted the bag on his shoulder and walked down the street, as instructed. Coal Miners were used to walking with their heads down, but Will found it difficult to keep from gawking. The new sights of the city were a wonder to Will and the enormity of the place made him feel like a little sparrow darting among crows.

Chapter Six

I took my time walking through the warren of streets in Central London. I managed to find my way to St Giles, but I wasn't ready to meet Aunt Betrys just yet. To be frank, the dimness, and the shock of the containment and the strange smells among the foggy brown haze made me heady. I needed to see a horizon so I kept on walking, through the Seven Dials, passing Covent Garden Market until I hit the Adelphi Terrace on the River Thames. I sat on the side wall that wrapped along the wharf, and cast my eyes over to the hubbub of carts and coaches clattering across Waterloo Bridge to my left. In front of me, coal was being unloaded from a lighter into a number of carts. As I watched the men unloading the coal, I felt this strange melancholy sweep over me.

So many men give their sweat for a cartload of coal. It's a strange thing, to consider the life of it. It lies in darkness, extracted, cleaned, counted, coined, cared for, carried away to cart and foreign coasts, and ultimately charred by the fire. So much effort in the act of nurturing something till it comes forth, a short burst of warmth, energy and heat that turns again cold, into white ash, a bright spark reduced to dust in the wind. I realised, looking back on that day, that the earth feasts on men as men feast on coal and I thank God the difference between me and a heap of coal is hope in life eternal.

As for my new life in St Giles, it was dubbed the 'Holy Land', and I can tell you straight, it bore no resemblance to the Promised Land by which God's Prophets foretold. Most of St Giles peoples were of Irish and Welsh blood; fleeing the famine in their lands only to find themselves still hungry with the added contempt of the well-heeled to add reproach to their poverty. St Giles was the heart of London, sixty-eight acres of black rot that ran south from Tottenham Court Road and Bloomsbury, Soho on its western edge with Seven Dials to the east.

For every thousand men, there was fifty privies, and for every fifty men there was one in employment. We was in the hungry forties. The Whigs had made it a crime for a beggar to find rest from his wretchedness in a public place. You see, it's not polite for posh folks to look out their parlors and to have to put up with seeing paupers. It puts them off their morning tea. They like to open the dailies by the fire, and read the yarns they tell each other about those in the cold – as it was considered

"So many men give their sweat for a cartload of coal. It's a strange thing, to consider the life of it. It lies in darkness, extracted, cleaned, counted, coined, cared for, carried away to cart and foreign coasts, and ultimately charred by the fire. So much effort in the act of nurturing something till it comes forth, a short burst of warmth, energy and heat that turns again cold, into white ash, a bright spark reduced to dust in the wind."

too dangerous to approach wretches - they was all lazy, drunk, thieving malcontents – so the stories went – and paupers deserved their plight – so they said.

It was a difficult time, being in London. I arrived in St Giles as a naïve youth, unsure of my place in the world. When the time came for me to go, I can say with certainty that I left St Giles a certified man... but I guess I'm getting ahead of myself again, as I am wont to do. You see, I was in search of Cherry Tree Lane - that was the address on the scrap of paper I had, where my Aunt Betrys lived, and for all my wandering up and down those awful alleys, and sagging houses and crowded courts, some with alleyways so cramped I had to walk in sideways, I couldn't find the street.

The sun had set about three hours prior and I had been walking all day. I was tired and hot, my feet hurt but the cold air kept me alert. I sat on a small bench, not knowing what to do next. I was on New Oxford Street, and it was lined with gas lamps that burned a strange muddy glaze due to the fogginess begging for warmth around its tepid blaze.

There was a lively coffeehouse opposite me, so I decided a bit of grub and a pot of coffee should set me square. I paused outside briefly, before entering the shop. It was a typical working class coffeehouse. A mish-mash of boxes and tables set irregular on scratched timber floors. There was a large open fireplace on the far back wall, with a thick iron bench over the fire, holding a line of hot iron kettles and big pots of pea and eel soup. Random stools was occupied by scruffy-looking boys, hot tea in their hands, with their back to the fire. There was people standing, and crowded around square tables, jugs of beer, hot elder wine and peppermint water, four penny plates of beef, hot potatoes with sticky gravy, penny loaves and chunks of cheese.

I stood, scanning the room for a nook to park me noodle and found none. A wizened waiter, with bright blue eyes and a shock of white hair and mustard neck tie wrapped tight around his neck approached me.

"Evenin. Eatin or drinkin boy?" asked the waiter.

"Some suppa and a hot tea Sir," replied Will.

"Follow me then."

The Waiter led Will to a table where a hunched over black man was dozing against the wall.

"Cuffay, you been hangin' onto that Everton Toffee like it's a hot tit for the past four hours. Time to move on, we got a payin' customer."

"No need," Will said quickly. "Happy for the company, if Sir don't mind."

"There we go then, boy's got manners. Pleased to oblige if you order me a finger thumb. It's me birthday and I'm in the mood for celebratin'," Cuffay lifted his empty cup and gestured for Will to sit down.

"Well it's your lucky day then ain't it Cuffay? Right. One cup O' rum for the bum, and what about you then Joskin?"

Will cleared his throat, "Ah, me name's Will. How much for taters and eel soup?"

"Well we is purists here, we don't mix our eels and tots. It's a ha' penny cupful of eel and 3d for two plates of tots."

"Aight," nodded Will.

"Right O then Joskin, a finger thumb for you too? Seein it's a celebration and all," said the Waiter.

"Ahh, yes. Yes two rums, for me and my…ah Cuffay." Will looked at Cuffay and counted his coin to pay the waiter.

"Do I look like a charity gala Joskin? You need to add a penny per plate – for me services."

"Ah. Sorry," Will handed over the three extra pennies.

"Right O." The waiter put the money in the front pocket of his long mustard-coloured smock and promptly walked off.

"So what brings you to this illustrious 'stablishment boy?"

"I'm movin' in with me Aunt Betrys," said Will, as he tried not to notice Cuffay hunched oddly over the table.

"Where's yer lodgin's? In the Rookery?"

"Well you see, I just arrived this mornin' and I can't find the street. I've been goin' round in circles for a ha'day. Cherry Tree Lane, you know it?"

" 'Aint ringing no tune," Cuffay looked around and yelled out to a tall lean man with dark hair. "Jacob! Jacob!" And he waved his hands for the man to come over.

Jacob approached the table. He had a square set jaw, with pale skin and pale blue eyes.

"Where's Cherry Tree Lane?" asked Cuffay.

"Who wants to know?" said Jacob.

"I just asked yer, didn't I?" Cuffay raised his thick black eyebrows.

Jacob laughed. "Well, you is about two years too late. It was one of them Streets raized for ventilation me boy."

"Ventilation?" swallowed Will.

"That's a fancy word for knockin' down a thousand cribs to make way for improvements – this spankin' street being one them newly ventilated."

"I don't understand," said Will. "Where do they go, then, if their houses are taken from them?" Will clasped his hands tightly under the table.

"Pollies call it progress boy. And they 'aint in the business of housin' the poor, they in the business of movin' 'em along," said Jacob.

"Well that 'aint right, what about me Aunt?" Will felt a rising panic and tried to remain calm.

"If it 'aint no concern to the City Gov'nr, what concern is it to you boy?" asked Jacob.

"Well. It 'aint…decent," insisted Will, despairing.

Jacob laughed. "Looks like we gotsa Devil-dodger in our midst. What's yer name?"

"Will."

Jacob stepped aside to let Walter the waiter place the tray of food and rum on the table. He grunted at Cuffay before walking off.

"Will 'aint got nowhere to lodge, Jacob. His aunt lived in Cherry Tree Lane," said Cuffay.

"What concern is that o' mine?" asked Jacob.

"Maybe yer need another waiter. God knows yer could do with someone a bit more amicable than that wet Walter White over there," said Cuffay loudly, nodding towards Walter.

"I flamin' heard that tailor," said Walter.

"Yer was meant to," said Cuffay.

"Yer a waiter Will?" asked Jacob.

"I'm a coal miner," said Will.

"Ain't no coal mine 'round these parts," said Jacob thoughtfully.

"I'd be grateful for a job, I work hard," said Will.

"Well tickle me trotters, I don't pay you a salary boy, you pay 1s a week for the privilege of workin' in me digs, and the patrons – the silk ties that they are – pay yer a penny per plate or more if yer powlite," said Jacob.

"Thank you Sir, I got 1s. I can start tomorrow," said Will, and he reached into his pocket and handed Jacob one shilling.

"Well, I wasn't expecting that," said Jacob. "I guess a deal's a deal then. Yer can sleep out back, there's a patch o' floor yer can grab some zees. We start at 3.30am. Day off for Sundee and I'll expect you'll be grateful seeing youse a devil dodger and all. There's the local lean 'n lurch down the road. You'll meet Kirk Keeper and Nikki Bag-blower soon enough." Jacob slapped the table and walked away.

Cuffay raised his chipped cup of Rum in the air. "Well yer ain't got no cherries, but at least yer landed yerself a bowl of sucked pips. Welcome to St Giles boy."

CHAPTER SEVEN

I never got to meet Aunt Betrys after all. In the first year of my lodging at Jacob's Coffeehouse, I made enquiries, here and there, leaving notes at the markets and corner stalls, but no one knew her. I wondered if she went by another name, but of course, as I had never met her, I had no way of describing her. She was a stranger to me too and all I had was her name and a street now buried. I eventually stopped asking and let God Almighty charter my course.

I spent hard days at Jacob's Coffeehouse. Every day had its own routine. There was three back rooms, the far room being mine and Walter's lodgings – we each had a narrow bed and a stool with the luxury of a candle and holder – it was my little corner of hope among mops and buckets and a shelving of linen. Walter was certifiably unhappy about this new development, and made his displeasure known by hanging up a sheet between his bed and mine. He kept mum for the first three months and I was happy to oblige his silence.

The room closest to the front of house, was where we did all the food preparation on a thick-set rough-hewn timber table. It had all sorts of nicks and ridges all crashing into each other and I often found myself running my fingers through the deep cuts in the timber, thinking about Dad. There was also four 110 gallon barrels filled with water stored side-by-side along the back wall. The water authority only turned the street tap on for two hours, every Tuesday and Friday only, so we was all out of our hovels, scurrying to and fro from kitchen to street corner, like rats in sunlight, filling up our barrels with buckets of wet goodness.

Every other day, except Sunday, we was woken by Traps on night watch. You see, in them days, we had no clocks. Traps, or Grunters as Jacob called them, were always dressed in long gray coats, slouch hats and a long sturdy baton in hand – they would call out the half hours on their patrol. For an extra bit of tin – and to help with community relations no doubt – you could pay a Trap a half deaner a week to bang a few curt raps on your door with his long baton, when you needs be woken up.

It took me a while, but as the city was always beaten a drum at any hour, there was a hierarchy of knocks one got nouse to. A postman would rap twice, loudly and quickly; an unexpected visitor was a feeble long knock. The Master of a house would knock loud and increase, until the servant announced the Master at the door to the rest of the inhabitants with a loud rap of bell inside. If you was a smithy of any trade, you had no door knocking privileges – all help was to deal directly with the kitchen ringing a bell on the side of the house. Footmen would rap with a sing-song tune that was in step with their livery – brassy buttons, braids, breeches and buckles.

Of course, none of that was any of my concern, only the 3.30am rap from Constable Haly – he would tarry until Jacob yelled out "Aight!" then he'd continue on his way.

The third room was Jacob's crib and I never saw inside, it being strictly off limits - until I had been at the Coffeehouse for nearly four years – but I will get to that soon enough.

Once woken, we three would quickly dress and hurry with large sturdy sacks and wheelbarrows to Covent Garden Markets. The best pickings were gone before dawn so Jacob was always eager like to fill up our sacks with the specials of the day. All the market gardens costermongers, particularly south of the river, would sell their offerings here. Traffic from 2.30am onwards into and out of Covent Gardens was lively. It was so large, it spread for hundreds of yards in all directions, from Long Acre to the Strand, from Bow Street to Bedford.

Ladies carrying heavy loads of produce on heads, men moving carts full of goods, coffee stalls, potato stalls, butchers and livestock, vegetables, fruits and fish all linin' the pavement on either side, stored up in heaps, moving between cart and wooden shed to the kitchen-hand's spoon.

Saturday was the busiest and best day of the week, as Jacob would let us sit, for an hour after our buying, in the coffee stall where he bought the week's coffee for the shop. The sun would just be rising and he'd shout us a hot brew – split pea or everton toffee – with a hot loaf and chunk of cheese and I would just watch the people, bustling about, peering over my tea, imagining I was dressed like a downy jagger with time to trade.

I liked Jacob. He didn't talk much, but when he did, it meant something. He reminded me of my Dad.

Once we returned to the shop, usually an hour after dawn, we'd be preparing the food for the day. The cook - Dr Berry we called him - as he was partial to dissecting and discussing the anatomy of the animal we was serving for the day – always arrived straight after we'd return from the markets. He used to go with Jacob and Walter to Covent Garden, but since I arrived, Jacob told him that he's too old and the

*"The sun would just be rising and he'd shout us a hot brew — split pea or
everton toffee — with a hot loaf and chunk of cheese and I would just watch
the people, bustling about, peering over my tea, imaging I was dressed like
a downy jagger with time to trade."*

cold 'ain't kind to infirmities. Dr Berry looked about a hundred years old, but he was nimble for an old fella. Of course, Jacob meant well, but Dr Berry didn't take too kindly to this new development either. I kept my shirt tucked in and my own counsel, trying me best to come to the mark on any instruction.

He would inspect the food, separating portions according to the menu for the day – and then he would bark in his gravely voice, "Chop this! Dice that! Wash this! You missed this here! Stoke the fire! Get out of my way!" so Walter and me would scurry along, basically doing whatever the old cook said.

Once all pots was simmering' then High Toby would take over as kitchen-hand and helping Dr Berry throughout the day's service. I guessed that he was a little older than me. He was short and scrawny, a jumpy kind of fella with a thick matt of hair tucked under a brown cap he always wore. I could hardly understand a word he said, as his words all ran into each other. He was always darting around, hopping and nacking about some highway robber in his collection of penny dreadfuls. Cuffay told me that High Toby had lofty aspirations, wanting to be remembered alongside the likes of Dick Turpin and Jonathan Wild. I thought Toby's ambition was a peculiar one, but like Dad used to say, every man has his direction to which he turns.

Once High Toby took over, Walter and me would prepare the linen and set the front of house, ready for the day's patrons. Jacob gave me a loan, letting me buy me own linen and cups as Walter was not partial to sharing his stash. All linen and cups were the keep and responsibility of the waiter, not the owner of the shop.

Jacob's Coffeehouse was open from ten to ten, six days a week, and open on Sundays after 2pm, once the Midday service at the St Giles Church had finished.

Most shops closed on Sundays, for the appearance of propriety rather than piety as most fellas and young kids holding big jugs to fill up with ale for the Sunday meal was yabbing outside, waiting for the pubs and gin houses to open after the end of Sunday Mass.

The residents of St Giles also needed to eat, as we was all scraping by, no one stored food in their lodging – it being conducive to vermin and the like and no room for storage, mostly everyone ate out on the streets - either on their way to work or on their way home - at chophouses, coffeehouses or corner stalls.

Jacob's Coffeehouse, being somewhat large and light on the tin, was the heart of St Giles.

Of course, Kirk the Keeper, the Parishioner at St Giles Church – or

"Cuffay told me that High Toby had lofty aspirations, wanting to be remembered alongside the likes of Dick Turpin and Jonathan Wild. I thought Toby's ambition was a peculiar one, but like Dad used to say, every man has his direction to which he turns."

as Jacob called it – the Lean 'n Lurch – would argue otherwise. He was a kind, funny middle-aged fellow, unmarried, and often quoted from the likes of Ezekiel and Jeremiah, given the temperament of occasion or when a solemn word was warranted.

Kirk found patronage at St Giles Church inconsistent. It was of an Anglican flavour in the middle of a Catholic Burrough – St Giles being mostly Irish immigrants loyal to their brand of gospel.

After the great fire of 1666, Parliament ordered fifty new churches to be built in part to replace those lost in the fire. It was in a way, just another slight to the people of St Giles to build an Anglican rather than a Catholic Church. My dad used to say that people who had a voice felt it convenient to speak on behalf of those who had no voice.

I liked Kirk. He always ordered everything separately so I could earn more money per plate. Every day he ordered a serve of eggs, tots and tea with two slices of bread 'n butter.

Kirk was often accompanied by Nikki the Bagblower – she didn't say much, but she always ordered cold sausages and would play the bag-pipes at funeral processions and weddings. It was highly irregular to have a lady piper, but she played so damn fine, everyone gave pardon to convention. She would tame her red curly hair under a dark blue bonnet and a matching shawl was always over her shoulder. She was part of the women's committee at the Church. She was always helping the street kids and knocking on doors and putting on stalls to raise funding for Matron Aimee, the teacher at the Ragged School nearby. Both was fine ladies.

Then there was the Hellite, Mr Oronoker who was a dab at poker. I admit I was a little scared of his fierce craggy countenance, with his sharp black eyes and hawkish nose, but he was a good tipper – most gamblers was generous when they is in a flush, so it made one amenable to small favours when they was in a straight.

St Giles was my place, Jacob's Coffeehouse my home, and my daily regulars was my people. One day, early Sunday morning in February 1848, all these people, in a very real way, became like blood to me.

CHAPTER EIGHT

Knock, knock. "Aight?"

"Jacob, it's me Gethyn. You said you wanted to see me before I knock off?"

"Come in."

I opened the door and looked shyly around Jacob's crib. It was the first time I had been invited into his room and I was fretting, wondering what this meeting was about. A large window on the southern side let in shafts of warm early morning light over Jacob's desk. His room had a quiet air about it. A small dark woolen red rug with long frayed ends laid between the iron bed and the desk under the window. It was the only item that gave an otherwise stark room a curt welcome. There were piles of books and papers on Jacob's desk. Jacob sat intently over his papers, and motioned with his hand for me to sit down on one of the chairs opposite his desk.

Jacob looked up from his desk and smiled.

"Kinchen. Young Will Gethyn. Yer been with me for a while. Seen things. Heard things," said Jacob.

"I dunno Sir. Got a bridle on me east and south," said Gethyn.

"Now, that's why I like yer Kinchen. Yer ain't one to blow the gaff." Jacob paused. "No doubt you've heard a lot of rumblin' this past year around the coffeehouse."

"Sir?"

"I know yer ain't no whiddler Kinchen. Unleash them whids now boy. I want to know what yer think about all the goings on here with O'Connor and the like."

"Well. It seems that folks are mighty excitable. O'Connor's got a gift of nabbin' it. I enjoy hearin' him talk," said Will reservedly.

"Now that King Phillippe's lost his knickers... it's a victory for the workers in froggesville, it's a sign that we're ripe for a win on this side of the straight. I know youse ain't no fresh gush Kinchen. A man who keeps his own counsel don't mean he ain't got nothin' to say. O'Connor's visits this past year ain't cause he's partial to Dr Berry's pickled plums. The Irish Feds of this illustrious quarter – of which I'm Guv, entered into an alliance with O'Connor's mob. Now I want to know, whether you're stayin' on the cart or we needs be dropping yer off at the next turnpike," said Jacob.

Tensions had been peaking at the coffeehouse for the past 18 months. Even Kirk the Keeper had little standing room at his Sunday sermons now. Nikki would play the pipes at the end of the service – as it were, a type of rally cry, as the folks squeezed out all quarters after morning mass to get a seat at Jacob's Sunday roast – which was essentially a town hall style meeting with shoe shiners and cabinet makers, carpenters, tailors, silk-weavers, and all the trades in-between. With the front windows' curtains drawn, Jacob would usually open the roast with a reading from the latest issue of the Northern Star – a monthly mouthpiece of the working poor's struggle against eating from an empty bowl.

Times weren't just tough for St Giles and the Seven Dials. All over London and in the provinces, from North England, East Midlands, The Potteries, The Black Country and South Wales, workers was brewing a heady rage – the kind of white hot heat that comes from years of containing anger deep inside the bowels. You see, that's the thing about change. It never comes about as the result of an isolated incident. It's a combination of competing and parallel factors over time that coincide to produce enough pressure to erupt into violent confrontation. No different to how time and pressure makes coal. No different at all.

It's a queer thing about London. It's disparate boroughs, while conjoined by boundaries, were separate in spirit. Each borough had no concern for the goings on with folks in the next quarter as we was all busy avoiding a hungry death. London seemed too large, too complicated, too diverse for any kind of collective voice… until now. It seems that poor folks had found a name to unite their dissatisfaction – they called themselves Chartists. Of course, the young lads had no real inkling of what it meant in terms of political life or its particulars in regards to constitutional pleas for male suffrage. For the illiterate on the street, it was a promise of employment, better wages, cheaper bread and baccy, and a dignity to be desired by a future wife. After all, it's hard to for a man to have a sense of decency if he can't find the means to mend his only pair of boots.

For the past two decades, the working poor bore the burden of the city's advancements. With lodgings being razed to make way for railways, docks or new streets, the poor was compensated with an eviction notice and less work. With the financial crisis that hit London last year, many landowners went bankrupt and workers had to hang up their belts in the building trades. You see, opportunities in London for the working class was mostly seasonal. Most folks was reliant on the downy folks visiting London for the social season from April to August.

They'd rent fancy cribs and hire the likes of us domestic dirt bags to wipe their chins and asses while their daughters with swelling breasts were primed and paraded to eligible suitors in matrimony – and so the cycle of privilege was assured.

The passing of the hated Reform Act and the Poor Laws a decade earlier, kept the poor moving on and their kids out of school, as families constantly migrated for work. The fact that the working poor had no chance of property ownership, or political voice meant that the privileged suffered no respite for the poor. Even in death, we was guaranteed an equal discomfort – as we was tossed on top of each other in barely open graves.

And now that the insurrection had happened in Paris, and similar spot fires had erupted elsewhere in Europe, O'Connor was the focus, the medium, in which the hungry Londoner could be channeled and heard. I was only seventeen, but I understood what Jacob was asking of me. I would have been no different to any other street Arab if he hadn't taken me in three years ago.

"Whatever you need Jacob, you'll find me willing," said Will.

"Pleased to hear it Kinchen. O'Connor and Lovett are hosting today's roast. Should be a good turnout. Get the water on the boilers, we open shop in thirty minutes."

Will nodded and got up to leave.

"Oh, and Kinchen... tell Dr Berry to cut yer a slice of his apple pie."

Will smiled. "Thanks Guv." He closed the door behind him.

* * *

When Walter finally opened the doors of Jacob's Coffeehouse that Sunday, the news of O'Connor and Lovett's visit had drawn so many people, that Walter opened all the windows so the crowd on the street could hear them speak.

Dr Berry was beside himself, losing his handle at High Toby, who struggled to keep up with the dishes. The place was electric, the patrons were rowdy and the beer flowed. Caps were tipped and petticoats fluttered. Tin went into aprons, and sausages and tots, and tea and fat white loaves were placed on tables with a rare flourish from Walter – a penny a plate on a day like today was enough to coax civility from a starving rat.

Suddenly, a loud roar rumbled through the crowd outside, as O'Connor and Lovett inched their way through the boisterous mob. People was jostling to get in a personal greeting with O'Connor. There was plenty of "Oi O'Connor!" and "God be wi'd yer!" and "Here's the giant jagger!" He was more than a head above most of the crowd – a man famous for largess in physique as big as his rallies. His hands were like buckets, and his voice as deep as the Winstanley Pit.

After O'Connor served eighteen-months in the salt-box seven years earlier for the Newport Rising, his imprisonment anointed him as the unqualified leader of Chartism. He was adored by workers and feared by the Whigs.

Born in Ireland, O'Connor's celebrity was fever pitch in Central London. Over one hundred thousand Irish migrants lived in St Giles and Seven Dials, and O'Connor had a way of connecting with his own; they loved him and he loved them, and in their mutual love, they found respite. He couldn't push through the crowd, so Jacob passed a chair overhead and the crowd carried it along until it reached O'Connor. I will never forget the speech he gave that morning, as I stood on the perch of the coffeehouse watching him carefully place the chair on the ground and stand on the seat. He gestured for the crowd to be silent. A hush fell over the street as all eyes looked up expectantly.

"My brothers and sisters, I am here today, to remind yer that yer the lifeblood of this glorious city. For every five men, four of yer pull the chains of industry. For every three women, two of yer serve. And yet, while our wives' backs bend in the domestic services, and yer husbands' hands bleed serving God's country, the establishment would have us believe that our justifiable grievances, our demand for suffrage, our God given right to be treated equal under the law, makes us a threat to our beloved nations security.

Tell me, brothers and sisters, wives and daughters, sons and fathers, why should the cause for dignity bring us so much contention? Are we not all blood and flesh whether we be clothed in rags or finery? Are we not all subject to the common miseries regardless of the station we find ourselves born?

How long will we submit to this fable? How long will we endure the indignities of poverty that are thrust upon us by the very people who then despise us for the conditions of which we are forced to endure? Our Almighty God, the justest of judges, declared to men that we shall not have respect unto the poor or the rich man, but we shall judge with justice.

So tell me, brothers and sisters, where be this execution of justice for the workin' poor? We rise up early seeking justice, and go to bed left wantin'.

And it is this wantin', this deep need, that we all share, to simply

" I will never forget the speech he gave that morning, as I stood on the perch of the coffeehouse watching him carefully place the chair on the ground and stand on the seat."

seek a fair portion for our labours - to seek a voice in the country that we serve. For we are not an excessive people, and God Almighty who fills the heavens and earth is a witness to that.

So I ask you, brothers and sisters, to not bow your head in despair, but to remember yer rights for suffrage as a God-given right, and to lock arms with me, and to press forward again - like we do, time and time again.

When the reform act was thrown out of Parliament, and the Whigs betrayed us, we press forward.

When our rallies get disbanded and our sons and fathers are condemned to the salt-box for the cause of cheaper bread, we press forward.

When yer elected me Member of Parliament of Nottingham, and they sought to disqualify me, we press forward.

When we played by their rules, and established the Land Co-op seven years ago, that the workin' man may have a right to till his own soil and have a sense of dignity and purpose over the direction of his life, now, even now, my brothers and sisters, they seek to destroy and declare our fight for land ownership a lottery - and therefore, illegal. Yet we press forward.

Lock arms with me, brothers and sisters, and let us press forward again, in a multitude of strength - for we far outnumber those who oppress us.

Let us press forward and march together, to declare the Six Point Charter as a livin' testimony and witness against the gross injustice that is inflicted upon the workin' poor!

Let us press forward and cement April the tenth of 1848 as a day that the voice of the workin' man would not be silenced! For we will march on to Kennington Common as one voice, and deliver our petition to those who need to be reminded that it is the workin' poor that is the lifeblood of this glorious city! God be with us!".

Well I can tell you square, the crowd erupted into a maddened frenzy after O'Connor boomed that speech across St Giles. All the people chanted, "Slave-class nay more! Slave-class nay more! Slave-class nay more!".

In all my years, I do not recall ever feeling the way I felt that day. It must have been alike to the first time the city turned on the gas street lights. We all felt a sense of wonderment and hope for the future, that no matter what, we could press forward, and not forever be condemned to the damp darkness of a London night.

When the coffeehouse doors shut later that evening, the regular crew

"So tell me, brothers and sisters, where be this execution of justice for the workin' poor?
We rise up early seeking justice, and go to bed left wantin'. And it is this wantin', this
deep need, that we all share, to simply seek a fair portion for our labours -
to seek a voice in the country that we serve."

was there; Jacob, O'Connor, Lovett, Walter, Cuffay, Mr Oronoker the Hellite. High Toby and Dr Berry were finishing serving some grub for supper. I was busy making sure no top joint ran low, as Jacob always says an 'empty pint equals an empty till'.

Jacob slapped the table with a grin, "That was quite a musterin' O'Connor. What's yer take?"

"Aye, there's no drawin' it mild, it was heartenin' to see," said O'Connor.

Lovett ran his hands through his dark curly hair and sighed audibly before taking a swig from his mug.

"Lovett, yer been holding yer counsel all day, and for that yer are to be congratulated. But yer sighin' like a pent up Molly ain't gonna change what people want," said Cuffay.

"Indeed, Cuffay. Lovett here is no farkin' poker face," winked Mr Oronoker.

"Don't mistake my silence as me bein' dished. I still hold me ground - a show is all farkin' well, but it's a mistake to be thinkin' that a March is gonna change their minds. That kinda display will only cause them top hats to dig their heels in. What think yer? There ain't no Gov'nr that'll bend the knee by intimidation - whether they be one workin' man or a hundred thousand strong. To be sure, a March will get the attention to the cause, but it won't deliver what people want. We work through specific issues - through formal proceedings to legislative change. Chargin' head on to the state is a losin' battle. All change is through back-door wranglin' you know that full well," said Lovett.

"What would yer have us do Lovett? I can circulate fifty thousand copies of the Northern Star every new moon, howlin' about change, but it don't mean nothin' if we don't bare some teeth. Revolutions happen' all over Europe – as we speak. So if not now, when?" said O'Connor.

"Don't farkin' lecture me about barin' teeth. Yer sideshow is gonna undermine all the pavers that the NUWC have laid for the past eighteen years. The fellas at the union are not happy O'Connor.

Whatever squirrels we've managed to feed nuts inside in the Lower House, will farkin' run up the nearest tree with yer March. We'll get the signatures, to be sure, but we don't need a farkin' May Day with ribbons and fiddles makin' a ruckas. Yer just can't be patient can yer? It's all about yer farkin' ego. And it's gonna be the ruin of yer and others. Mark me words," said Lovett angrily as he looked around the room.

O'Connor stood up and leaned on his knuckles on the table in front of him. "Yer a farkin' armchair prognosticator Lovett. The NUWC would be nothin' without me holdin' rallies in the provinces for the past ten years and yer farkin' know it. So we'll see Lovett, we'll see. I'm goin' home," O'Connor grabbed his coat from the chair and left.

Lovett stood up. "There's plenty of ambitious men who've attached themselves to righteous causes for self-servin' reasons. Evenin' gentleman," said Lovett quietly and he left the room.

Jacob looked around room. "Aight farkas. Kitchen's closed."

* * *

It was fitting that the month of March was a flurry of activity to prepare for our march on Kennington Common in April. Lovett, O'Connor, Jacob and Cuffay was doing the rounds at every local Gin Palace, Penny Theatre and corner stores. They was hobnobbing with warehousemen, wharfingers, lightermen and coal stackers. At the directive of Jacob, me and High Toby was taking turns getting the petition signed and handing out NUWC flyers at every major turnpike into London. There was not a flyer that didn't go into the hand of every craftsman, shopkeeper, unskilled and skilled labourer, costermonger, apprentice and servant.

It wasn't always easy though. The toll gates wasn't just a gateway for workers passing through into town each day. It was also a place for plenty of marking by slops' spies and trappers waiting to nab frog and toe – which was essentially thieving folk scamps who'd come in and out of London. So any kind of loitering was not taken too kindly and we was often moved along by trappers after five in the morning. As most workers lived outside of London, we had to get to the turnpike real early, around four in the morning as many workers had to walk for up to two hours to arrive at their master's cribs by six. Early morning at the turnpikes also meant there were not likely to be slops hanging around, so we was able to get plenty of signatures before the sun broke through her veil.

After six in the morning, this was when all the stagecoaches and hackney carriages would pass through the toll gates, so it wasn't a good time to be hanging around on foot anyway. You see, most of them main roads was built by private coin who put up the tin to build the road, and in return, the whigs allowed them to levy tolls on all who passed through every gate; from the west in Knightsbridge, at Hyde Park corner, in Kensington, at the corner of the Earls Court Road, at Marble Arch, at Oxford Street, and in Notting Hill. On the north side of the city there was Kings Cross tollgate, and east at the City Road near Old Street, and at Shoerditch, in the Commercial Road. On the south side of London there was three turnpike gates in the Old Ken Road, another at the Obelisk at the Surrey Theatre, where Lembeth Road and St George's Road meet, with another at Kennington Church.

So High Toby and me, we each took turns, a turnpike each morning we did. We was fortunate though, as most toll-collectors was also sympathetic to the cause, so we could usually stay for an hour before the trappers arrived. Most toll-collectors wore a long white apron, with two large pockets in front, one on the left for holding tin, and one on the right for tickets; as a half-pence would buy you a 24-hour pass. This was why the trappers weren't too concerned about security between midnight and six; most of the traffic was croakers and workers; often too poor to pay the fee, so they'd often be let through a few days before pay day with a handkerchief, toothpicks or a piece of cutlery. We all knew that the cutlery would most likely have come from some master's scullery, but no one questioned the origin of the payment.

Beggars, or croakers as we called them, would hang around after six to offer water in buckets to the horses quickly during the short stop to pay before the coach moved along. The coach-driver often paid with a fresh chunk of bread. It was a system that worked I spose.

The price of bread was a constant preoccupation of the working poor. When the bread climbed higher than 11d a loaf, which was usually after a bad harvest, the impact on the street was devastating. Indeed, giving a chunk of bread to the poor became almost like a superstition among the wealthier folk, who'd often say, 'the blessing of cheap bread' when they'd throw a chunk to a beggar. It was a strange twist of logic that took too much emotion when one spent time dwelling on the dark irony of it all.

In the evenings, we was soliciting signatures at music halls and hanging around the exit doors of penny theatres. Once the show was finished, most of the folk went to their local gin palace – which was often next door to a music hall, so we made sure we had all angles covered.

London nightlife was always lively. There was all sorts of interesting molls, shicksters dodgers and duffers - the likes of which you'll always find loitering around theatres and music halls, selling glass baubles and scratchy handkerchiefs. There was also plenty of street fighters or nullin-coves they was called, who'd go to the music hall with a white chalky powder drawn around their eyes. We'd call them ebony optics albonised, cause the white would mask their shiners. There was also plenty of turkey merchants, the kind of folk that nab silk from weavers and on-sell it to the theatre holders for costumes and the like. You could always tell who they was cause they had a large black sack stuffed full of cloth on their backs.

"So High Toby and me, we each took turns, a turnpike each morning we did. We was fortunate though, as most toll-collectors was also sympathetic to the cause, so we could usually stay for an hour before the trappers arrived."

You see, them theatres and music halls and gin palaces, these were homes for most of the working poor as they shared their little crib with plenty of other poor folks, home was not a place to find solace. The music halls was a place one could sing about finding tin to pay the landlord, woe on heavy-handed husbands and cheating wives. There was ballads about Wat Tyler and other folk heroes. There was lots of poking fun at foreigners and plenty of songs that saluted mother England too. My dad used to say, that wherever there was hopelessness, you'd find patriotism hot and pungent. Cause most folks that aint' got no sense of pride in their living, have to make up a pride in their origin – gives 'em a sense of purpose. He always warned me to watch out for these kind of folks; not to get fooled; he'd say, "the ways of men are all strange before the Lord". I'll get straight to the mark, being out on a London night, this statement was on the square.

There was plenty of penny theatres in and around London too; in Covent Garden, Drury Lane, the Haymarket. The Coburg in Lambeth; the Surrey theatre only a few blocks away. The Bower also on the South Bank; the City of London in Shoreditch; the Standard in the same area; and the Pavilion in Whitechapel.

Mostly it was very young folk who went to the theatres. Chimney-sweeps, coal-heavers, slop-workers, scavengers, rubbish-carters and dustmen; all dressed in stained corduroy or fustian.

Being only 3d to see a show, the working poor would pass through sixty-thousand strong, standing in the pit each week for their weekly forgetment. It was a rowdy, and heady bunch, and sometimes the lack of elbow room caused fisti-cuffs during the end of year celebrations as patronage would nearly double; especially when Punch and Judy was on the night's ticket.

Gin Palaces was also plenty appealing too, being easy on the eye with pilasters and decorative cornices, carved balustrades and proud arched doorways. The dark was muted with gas fittings and it was a curious happening that the poorer the borough, the fancier the lush-crib. The bar was often French-polished mahogany and lushy-coves and molls would order rum shrubs, white satins, top joints and finger thumbs for a penny a glass. High Toby and me, we was going around the tables, popping flyers in pockets and petticoat's bonnets. We was leaving no coat unturned.

Even Kirk the Keeper and Nikki Bagblower was doing their part for the cause. They had the chartist hymn printed on the back of every flyer we handed out, and had the petition at the entry for signing each day. Matron Aimee and Nikki Bagblower would hold evening rehearsals

"My dad used to say, that wherever there was hopelessness, you'd find patriotism hot and pungent. Cause most folks that aint' got no sense of pride in their living, have to make up a pride in their origin – gives 'em a sense of purpose."

of our hymn and even the kid's parents from the Ragged School was soliciting signatures and sending them with the kids to school each day, to be collected by Matron Aimee and handed over to Kirk in the evenings.

The voices of this hymn in the early evening, with the bagpipes carrying its cry would resonate out the glazed windows of St Giles in the Fields and could faintly be heard by the more fortunate flock nearby, at St George's Church on Hart Street in Bloomsbury. On top of its spire stood a disproving statue of George I in Roman getup; as if the sound coming out of our Church was an affront to his dignity. It was no co-incidence to me that the St Giles in the Fields Church used to be a leper hospital seven hundred years ago. We was all broken in some way or another. The thing is, we was all poor, but that didn't mean we wasn't about to give up fighting for our dignity. That's what this March was about. In my mind, it was fighting the indignity of poverty. Well, you may as well be called a man without limbs if you can't feed your family and it was in the power of them queer-cuffins to give the people their limbs back...

CHAPTER NINE

"Well shite-bucket, nice to have yer over for an early mornin' everton toffee on yer big day," said Constable Haly.

"Yer can stop holdin' me hand yer treacherous slop. Don't want to waste me coffee on yer coat," said O'Connor as he yanked his arm out of Haly's grib. "What's the reason for the muscle then?" O'Connor looked around the empty pub. It was seven o'clock, Monday, April the 10th, the day of what came to be known as the last Chartist march.

"You, Mr O'Connor. You are the reason why I'm here, and I'm not pleased to be in your company either," said Sir Richard Mayne, the London Police Commissioner.

"Well, I is honoured to be in such decorated company. I'd love to hob-nob over tea and madeira, but I've got a charter to deliver to the houses of parliament today," said O'Connor.

"Quiet now," said the Commissioner.

Haly nodded and quickly drew his baton, winding O'Connor in the stomach with four sharp whacks of the rod. O'Connor fell to his knees with thud, and keeled over, gasping for air.

"Keep the rod on him Haly. From now on, this fat Irish prod is going to kneel, like all well-behaved bitches," said the Commissioner. "This moment O'Connor, is going to be the highlight of your career. The Prime Minister Lord John Russell, has asked me to deliver a message to you. This is the last time that Westminster will pay you any heed. We congratulate you on achieving quite a mustering today. What a shame your rabble won't be able to deliver your, no doubt, forged petitions to the houses of parliament".

"This is an infringement of the right of the people to petition parliament in person. Any opposition is highly illegal," grunted O'Connor.

The Commissioner raised his eyebrows, as Haly whacked O'Connor again. "Listen carefully O'Connor. You will tell your deluded rabble of 200,000 that they will not cross to the north bank. Nor will they force their way. In exchange, your Majesty will pardon your treason, and will not send you back to York Castle to serve time in jail, again. This time it won't be 18 months. It will be for life. There will be law and order in this metropolis, and there will not be another Newport Uprising".

O'Connor spat out blood before he spoke. "I have always been a man of peace. Moral force is the degree of deliberation in each man's mind which tells him when submission is a duty or resistance not bein' a crime. That true application of moral force would effect every change. But, if physical force comes to its aid, I'm just one man, what can I do to prevent it? God forbid I should want me country to plunge into horror of physical revolution, I've always wanted liberty won by peaceful means. Fark. That's what this March is all about," said O'Connor. "We don't seek violence. We seek suffrage for every workin' man as is our God-given right. Who are yer all to stand between a man and his rightful purpose?" said O'Connor.

"We have armed cavalry and infantry stationed on the south side of every bridge across the Thames. We have troops in reserve along the north side. Our steamboats hold 10,000 infantry, with loaded cannons near Buckingham Palace. Our soldiers are supported with 170,000 special constables, all with muskets, waiting to open fire, just like they did at Newport ten years earlier. Who are we, you ask? We are the keepers of law and order, boy. You may be able to arrange a good muster, but you are no descendant of an Irish king O'Connor, and this is not your land. You don't belong here. And you will die in jail for the murder of all those innocents that you've roused into a frenzy if you don't stand them down today. Her Majesty, in her grace and wisdom, will allow your illegitimate petition to be delivered, by the three stagecoaches that you have already hired, and you may accompany them. Just you. So you see, it's not all bad. You save face and the lives of those you've deceived," said the Commissioner.

"You cannae charge me with treason. I've not broken any law! Even if yer win today, and yer win again tomorrow, and the fella after yer bones have long turned to ash wins again, there will come a day when the people will say nay. Nay more. And they will rise up, in righteous indignation and there will be no measure to their fury. Come what may. That day will come, and men like yerself will wont a place to hide and yer will find no refuge from yer reckonin'," cried O'Connor.

"You're mistaken boy. Open and advised public speaking is now a treasonable crime. Her Majesty has ordered that the Crown and Government Security Act be written onto the statute book as we speak. It is retrospective. Anyone caught doing so will be arrested and charged with treason," said the Commissioner with a curt smile. "You can see how gracious Her Majesty is being towards you, by granting you this very generous foreword warning. So, what say you?"

For all his life, O'Connor was fighting everyone. The system, his father, the house of lords that stood between him and his dream of emancipation. Fighting for his position in The Working Men's Association, fighting to be loved back by the women who'd rejected him. Fighting with the bottle. Fighting to be heard by anyone who'd care to listen. Kneeling there, with the baton pressed hard at the nape of his neck, O'Connor felt his heart snap in defeat. He let out a long, deep howl.

The commissioner pulled out his handkerchief and threw it on the floor at O'Connor's knees. "Now that's a good dog. You see that Haly? When a dog is cornered, he will still fight to preserve his flesh. Few will ransom their flesh for honour. Get him out of my sight."

* * *

By the time Jacob locked up the coffeehouse doors at seven o'clock in the morning, the streets was already full of roughs walking to each of the four mustering points; east division on Stepheny Green at 8 o'clock; City and Finsbury division on Clerkenwell Green at 9 o'clock; west division in Russell Square at 9 o'clock, and the south division in Peckham Fields at 9 o'clock. The NUWC had appointed three leaders to head the march from each division, before proceeding all together onto Kennington Common.

Cuffay, O'Connor, Lovett, and Jacob's crew, we was all meeting up at Kennington Common directly as the petition, on the square to be sure, was nearly five-million signatures strong filling three hired stagecoaches, ready to be delivered across the bridges leading into Westminster by the working poor, for the working poor. So Jacob, High Toby, Walter White and me, we stepped out onto New Oxford Street and joined the tide of excitement that nudged us along to south of the Thames river.

It was an uncharacteristically warm day, Monday usually being besotted by a light drizzle to mourn the working week, but spirits were high, and the air felt light, with spring in full display in planter boxes beneath shopfronts, and lodgings' windows. No matter how poor one was, spring in London was always a time of a proud display of colour after a long dark winter. Hellebores, with their dark leathery leaves and little white flowers, sweet purple violets and red and yellow polyanthus, and pink and white heather, all was a sweet parade, cheering us along towards a hopeful victory.

When we arrived at Kennington Common, just before ten o'clock, we snaked our way to the stagecoaches, where Lovett and Cuffay stood, with other heavies from the NUWC.

"Cuffay, fine day for a revolution. That's quite a stacked rumble-tumble yer got there," said Jacob nodding to the stagecoach. "Where's O'Connor? Thought he'd be in the thick of the push by now."

"We haven't seen him. He was meant to be here at ha' eight. No doubt yer eyeballed them trappers? Seems like Her Majesty was prepared for some rat 'n cat. Folks are sayin' that plenty of conks sold out, and was sworn in as special cunnies – there's tens of thousands of 'em. See them conks with the truncheons and white arm bands? Farkas," says Cuffay.

"There is also calvary on the south and north side of the river Jacob. Heigh. Heigh! They've blocked every entry point at all the bridges too; can't see us muscling over Old Westminster, Blackfriars or the Hungerford. Where the fark is O'Connor? This is his farkin' weddin' day afterall," said Lovett.

"Aight, me peepers spy the mouthy-cove! There's O'Connor!" pointed High Toby excitedly.

"Farkas. About time," said Cuffay.

As O'Connor approached, it was clear that he wasn't looking too well.

"Sorry I'm late. Been doin' some recon," said O'Connor as he smiled weakly.

"Farkas. No doubt yer seen all them white bands with barkin' irons? Didn't know Her Majesty had such a farkin' surplus of armory," said Jacob. He looked closely at O'Connor. Yer is a queer-mollisher. You look like shite," said Jacob.

"Rough night," said O'Connor.

"Of all nights, ya lushy-cove," said Lovett.

"Listen, Cuffay, I want you to do the speech today. I'm sick of hearin' me own voice," said O'Connor.

Cuffay looked at Lovett.

"Sure, no problem with me," smiled Lovett.

"Okay, fine. We'll both do it. I'll gee em up, and you can finish em off Lovett. Let's go rum up the crowd!" grinned Cuffay. He climbed up onto the stagecoach and started waving his hands over his head. "Brotha slaves! Brotha slaves! Brotha Slaves!" Cuffay called out to Nikki the Bagblower nearby. "Blow yer mag Nikki! Let's get the rabble on!"

Nikki nodded and blew a long deep note on her bagpipes. The crowd erupted into a raucous cheer and roar and started singing the hymn that Kirk had printed on all the flyers -

"Brotha slaves! Brotha slaves! Brotha Slaves!" Cuffay called out to Nikki
the Bagblower nearby. "Blow yer mag Nikki! Let's get the rabble on!"

The Charter is our aim;
We claim it as our right;
Our ancient sires enjoyed the same
Nor feared oppression's might.

Then let us persevere
In such a glorious cause;
Let each demand a Briton's share
in making Britain's laws.

The laws you must obey,
Though made by cruel men;
And all unrighteous taxes pay,
Or fill the felon's den!

Fear not the hate of man -
God will your guardian be!
If you pursue the glorious plan
Of human liberty!

Men of England, ye are slaves,
Bought by tyrants, sold by knaves;
Your's the toil, the sweat, the pain,
Their's the profit, case, and gain.

Men of England, ye are slaves;
Beaten by policemen's staves;
If their force ye dare repel,
Yours will be the felon's cell.

Men of England, ye are slaves; -
Hark! the stormy tempest raves -
'Tis the nation's voice I hear,
Shouting, 'Liberty is near!'

A time for all to blend
Their energies and might!
For minor differences to end
In one grand point of right!
For knowledge, pure, refined,
To illumine every brow!
A time for every one inclined
To be a Chartist now!

Cuffay raised his arms for the cheers to die down after the hymn had ended. A hush fell over the crowd.

"Welcome Chartists, the Trades, The Irish Confederates, Repeal Bodies, my fellow brotha slaves. I stand here before you, a West Indian man. A lover of liberty. And I would dishonor human nature if I did not show myself a friend to the liberty of others. I am depicted as a hunchback monkey by the press. I am the son of a slave. The press misrepresent and vilify us and our intentions. Our grievances are deep! Our demands are just! Our families pine in misery, want and starvation! Today, we stand here, ready to press forward and demand a fair day's wage for a fair day's work! We are the slaves of capital - we demand protection to our labour. We are political serfs - we demand to be free. It is for the good of all that we seek to remove the evils from under which we groan. Brotha slaves! Brotha slaves! Brotha slaves! I congratulate the heroism of our brothers in France, and the proclamation of the second republic. If the Republic be for France – then let the Charter be for England! What say yer?" shouted Cuffay.

The crowd indeed went into a frenzy, shouting, "Republic for France, Charter for England! Republic for France, Charter for England!"

Cuffay motioned again for them to be silent.

"We have arrived at a time when a league of kinds is no longer to be dreaded. Never despair of yer rights, my brotha slaves. The day is no longer distant. The Charter must become the law of the land today! When we reform our electoral system, our suffering will be no more! Let me introduce to you, the author of our magna carta, William Lovett of the London Working Men's Association!"

The crowd started chanting, "Lovett! Lovett! Lovett!"

Lovett climbed onto the top of the second stagecoach and waited for the crowd to silence before he spoke.

"This Six Point Charter was first launched in Glasgow in May 1838, at a meeting attended by 150,000 honest, working men. The following year, we brought it to London with over one million two hundred signatures. Yet, the Houses of Parliament would not hear it. Ten years later, we stand here again. This time with nearly 200,000 people, and over five million signatures. Today, they will hear the voices of the lifeblood of our nation that demands universal suffrage. We demand a vote for every man twenty-one years of age, of sound mind, and without criminal conviction. We demand a vote by secret ballot so no tenant or employee can any longer be intimated at our hustings. We demand no property qualification. Whether a man be landed or not, let the quality of the man's virtue, not the size of his assets determine his fitness as a member of parliament.

"What about the size of his gonads Guv?" yelled a voice from the crowd which erupted into cheers.

"Well now, that for his missus to weigh," said Lovett. "We demand annual parliaments to rid our system of graft and intimidation by the incumbent. Let us make each ensuing a twelve monthly, so constituents will not be betrayed by their representatives in power. We demand equal representation, whereby the division of the Kingdom must be three hundred electoral districts, each containing an equal number of inhabitants, with no more than one representative from each district to sit in Parliament. Let's stop smaller constituencies swamping the votes of larger ones! Lastly, we demand the payment of members an annual salary of £500 so he may attend to the best interests of his country without compromising his family's livelihood. This Six Points Charter will return to each man his right to a fair day's wage for a fair day's work. Let's press forward together, and let the Houses of Parliament know that the working poor are united as one, and stand as one voice, with one purpose, under one God!" shouted Lovett as he raised his arm and pointed towards Westminster Bridge.

The crowd roared and pressed towards the north bank bridges. As Cuffay and Lovett climbed off the stage coaches, muskets were raised on the Westminster bridge and a caller yelled, "Make ready! Present! Fire!" as shots unloaded into the air, the crowd screamed and ran in every direction.

Cuffay started shouting, "press forward! Press forward towards the bridge! They is only trying to scare yer! Press forward damn it!"

"No! Disband! Disband! Get the hell out of here!" Shouted O'Connor.

Cuffay shouted at O'Connor in disbelief. "Are you out of yer farkin' mind? Them barkin' irons are just for show. Stow yer mag!"

O'Connor ignored him. "Get the fark out, Disband! Disband!" and he started shoving the men in front of him. "They will shoot. Don't stay here!" shouted O'Connor.

Cuffay was beside himself in fury. "No! 'On the slops! On the slops! He yelled as some people lurched forward towards the bridge, while others was running to get off the grounds.

Will was frightened and stood unsure. He turned to Jacob. "What do I do?"

"I think it's time to cut yer lucky," said Jacob quickly. "Grab Toby and get out of here farkin' quick".

"Aight. What about you?" asked Will.

Before Jacob could answer, a heavy baton came crashing down

"We are the slaves of capital - we demand protection to our labour. We are political serfs - we demand to be free. It is for the good of all that we seek to remove the evils from under which we groan."

on Jacob's head, crushing his skull. He fell to the ground, and died instantly. A riot had broken out and was spreading like wildfire through the crowd.

Will started screaming and rushed towards the trapper. Before he could lunge at the man who had killed his only friend, he felt a baton crack across the back of his head. His whole body went into a cold rush before he passed into blackness.

Cuffay went in a frenzied rage. He pulled a knife he had hidden in his boot and rushed towards a trapper, cutting him deep into the arm. Another constable grabbed Cuffay by the hair and knocked him to the ground, placing cuffs on his back.

As he was being arrested, the constable shouted, "you are under arrest for violating…" before he could finish, Cuffay shouted, "Speak no more Trapper! As I am a Chartist, I understand it".

CHAPTER TEN

The riot on Kennington Common was quickly subdued. By two o'clock the entire area was empty, save the discarded, sodden flyers littered about the ground. Nearly twelve thousand, coordinated arrests were made, many of them Chartists' and Irish Confederates' leaders, including Will. By early evening, Lord John Russell was able to certifiably report to Queen Victoria, "to the full credit of the crown and country" that the march was an abject failure.

Under armed guard, O'Connor escorted the petition-filled coaches across the Westminster Bridge to the Houses of Parliament. Curiously to the public, but not of course to O'Connor, and to his great shame and relief, he was neither arrested nor detained at the Old Bailey, awaiting trial for sedition and treason with many others.

There was scattered demonstrations in London, around Clerkenwall Green, which continued for the next month, but the voices of resistance eventually went underground and was stilled.

The petition was unanimously defeated by Parliament. After less than a day's deliberation, clerks declared less than two million signatures illegitimate, not that the impossibility of such a quick turnaround was questioned publicly. The working poor understood all too well, that this was not the season in which victory would be assured. The women continued to give suck to new babes, and the working man pressed on, waiting for his due. There was however, a curious sign, which confirmed in the people's minds that the Good Lord looked down and saw the affliction of the oppressed. Indeed, the day Parliament rejected the People's Charter, it was unearthed that the new Houses of Parliament had defective sewers. The stink was so bad, that many members refused to leave their country homes until it was fixed months later.

It was a reproach that the pride of London was sitting atop a great cesspool of shite, with the main sewer running underneath the entire length of the building. The air was so foul when the pipe was dug, every flaming lamp put out its light. The pipe was laid crooked so the shite couldn't drain away...by then of course, it was too late. The rank system set off a cholera and typhoid outbreak, and the poor was to be subdued again.

Many of the prisons only had a fifteen hundred men capacity.

With the influx of all the rioters, the prisons was grossly overcrowded, making it ripe to disease spreading. In those few months, most of the rioters died in prison. For the blinded hearts, they saw an unjust calamity, but for those who walked with their Maker, they understood that there was life in retribution. The young men who died fighting for what was right, suffered a short exile on earth before being translated. As I sat in Newgate Prison, witnessing the devastation around me, I saw the meaning of what my Dad used to recite to me, of the Wisdom of Solomon, being played out before me eyes –

"The souls of the righteous are in the hand of God, and there shall no torment touch them. In the sight of the unwise they seemed to die and their departure is taken for misery, and their going from us to be utter destruction: but they are in peace. For though they be punished in the sight of men, yet is their hope full of immortality. And having been a little chastised, they shall be greatly rewarded: for God proved them, and found them worthy for Himself. As gold in the furnace hath He tried them, and received them as an whole burnt offering".

It was a strange twist of irony that the prisoners who volunteered to work in the infirmary had their sentences remitted and even earnt some tin, while the Chaplain refused to conduct a funeral service over the wretched of the earth – he would stand afar reading dust to dust – before dropping his handkerchief to the ground.

Who can guess at the wrath of our Maker on the day of vengeance against the hypocrites. God help us all.

* * *

Aight. The traditions of men. It is a mask that brings comfort and terror, depending on the circumstance you find yourself in. The pleasure of knowing what to say, how to behave, who to respect – is also played out in our deepest fears too. So when the bell tolls from the belfry at St Sepulchre at midnight, all inhabitants at Newgate Prison know that this is the sound of the last sunrise for those sentenced to hang at Tyburn, two o'clock, sharpish.

If a condemned man was standing here, he would tell you that certainty of death has a smell. Whether you're a Tip-topper bleeding on silk sheets, or a wretched cull among other wretches sharing an eight feet by six cell, the smell of the grave fills all men's senses. Damp. Acrid. Wet shite in a windowless room, suffocating thick dirt down a scratchy throat. If a baby could talk, he would tell you it's the same smell coming into the world as when you know you're about to leave it.

*"For the blinded hearts, they saw an unjust calamity, but for those who walked
with their Maker, they understood that there was life in retribution. The young
men who died fighting for what was right, suffered a short exile on earth
before being translated."*

Newgate or The Whit as it was called, (in honour of Dick Whittington's cat smirking macabre-like at the foot of its pilaster), was a five-storey high confinement of human misery. Restored after the great fire of 1666, its grand exterior could not detract from the foul odours of life in a space where the doctors too forgot their oaths to treat its ailing malefactors.

But life goes on inside, human nature's proclivity to carry on, being as it was, women was still wives to their men, children was born and fed here. There was order among turmoil; the Keeper's Lodge, where bub, grub and baccey could be bought for less than a rogue n' villain. The Master's side, where common charity wards house up to thirty prisoners per room, and the Press-Yard where prisoners commune by day - a shadowy space of blank stone walls that spat out black angry spikes into the sky.

Will stared out into the darkness, pressing his forehead between the cool iron bars of his cell. He shared the room with two others, who both now lay, huddled together on a rope mat, sharing two stable rugs. Newgate was famous for its special brew to help keep the prisoners warm at night. Affectionately coined kill-grief, cock-me-cap, poverty or meat and drink by its grateful loyalists, it was a mean gin that punched a good fight against an unforgiving cold stone floor.

His cellmates, knowing it was Will's last night before his hanging, expected he may want a final hurrah, as was the custom among the condemned; they talked trash most the night, begging him to hand the turnkey his rhino, sink his morgan rattler into a mawkes' cuckoo nest, tell the devil-dodger when he comes knocking for Will's last rites to bowl away the queer-cuffin's peepers and wake up just in time to dance the Paddington frisk to cheers of his fellow men below the gallows... But Will would have none of the malarkey. Will was tired. He sat, unspeaking by his cell's window - a hole in a three-feet-thick front wall, crossed by two frames of jealous iron bars. His cellmates, respecting his want for privacy, got sewed up and fell asleep as soon as poverty laid her thick veil across their shrunken skulls.

Will looked up at the near full moon, high above. "Mr Oliver," he said under his breath, so High Toby used to call it. His gaze followed downward, across Skinner Street to St Sepulchre's belltower. He could hear echoes of steps from the night watchman and see the light from his lantern dance unnatural shadows through the small stone windows of the belltower room. So, it was time.

A peal of twelve deep tolls resonated across the courtyards. When the last echo died, a low voice, rehearsed in his victual to the valley of the vanquished slowly began –

"All you good people, pray heartily unto God for these poor sinners, who are now going to their death, for whom this great bell doth toll."

The watchman paused and then drew in a deep breath, quickening his pace-

"All you that in the condemned hold do lie,
Prepare you, for tomorrow you shall die.
Watch all, and pray, the hour is drawing near,
When you before the Almighty must appear.
Examine well yourselves, in time repent,
That you may not to eternal flames be sent."

In the cell next to Will, a shrill voice called out through the bars, "Mr Bellman! Call for a pint! When I was in a good dress, I'd charge a sovereign! Now five to ten shillin' for a poke! Farkas!" the woman sobbed.

Will turned away from his window, his face contorted. He blew out the candle. He sat upright, still for a few moments, as if undecided, before lying down on his hand-hewn mat, pulling the filthy rug up over his ear.

* * *

Jonah Cotton didn't start out life wanting to be a man of the cloth. It just so happened that way, and he's not the kind of man who likes to divulge particulars about the how and the what, so we'll never know just how he ended up being the Chaplain of Newgate Prison or what he did to be posted there. Nonetheless, his superiors measured his worth by how quickly he was able to break the spirits of the capitally convicted so they would meet the hangman in resignation, rather than resistance.

The 'breaking in' was a carefully protracted spectacle, beginning with the Queen in Council's recorder's report to the condemned; a lottery registrar of the Queen's clemency. Out of twenty convicted, five may receive a royal pardon, and for the remaining sentenced to hang, up to three names will draw a blank, meaning death. It was never a case of the blanks being guiltier than others, but one of providence. After delaying the recorder's report till after supper, Jonah would address the prisoners with the news. The crowd's reaction was mixed.

"Yer farkin' ass twitch, I'll slit yer throat for keeping us in suspense for so long!"

"God have mercy!"

"Beezelbub's rodent!

"See all yer spooney gorgers in hell first!"

Jonah would leave the yard as soon as the last name had been read, leaving the prisoners to act out scenes of wild despair, jealousy, rage, secret relief or stupefaction. The guards would then herd the convicted into their cells, for a night of sleepless terror or thankful slumber. The very next day, the newly condemned were escorted to the Prison Chapel and seated on a black painted pew below the pulpit. An open coffin was strategically placed at the centre table. After every Old Bailey session, they would sit on their pew, while respectable ladies and gentleman would pay tickets for the best view; the sheriff would wear his gold chain and the whole congregation would rise and sing praise, before the Chaplain began his service.

Jonah, gifted in the art of rhetoric, would weave his words to captivate and terrorise his audience, covering the entire gamut of divine wrath, shame, orphans and widows, to suffering and wretchedness. The first sermon of this type would give Jonah a good indication on who would be a hard nut to crack. The screamers, the head smackers and the silent sobbers could pretty much be left to their own devices. By the end of the week, these types are wide-eyed obedient, contrite. As for the ones whose eyes turn a vacant madness, they are unpredictable yes, but generally, give over to the hangman with a lot of talk but little fuss. The ones he had to 'work' was those who sat still, defiant. Unblinking. Thankfully, it was usually only one or two of these that needed his full attention.

Will Gethyn was one such charge.

During the course of his six-week incarceration at Newgate, his seventeen years did not match the years on his face, but Will gave nothing of his heart, preferring to keep his own counsel during Jonah's sessions with him.

Sighing, Jonah held his lantern in front of him, as he walked the dark passage to Will's cell. As is the custom, after the bellman tolled, the Chaplain would visit the defiant.

The Guard, seated, nodded. "Evening, it's a bright moon tonight Reverend".

"Good evening. Let me in to see Will."

"As you wish." He stood up, stretching, careful to disguise a yawn with a cough. He turned the rusted key into the grill lock and the door creaked open.

"Get up Will, you've got a visitor," the guard barked.

Jonah stepped into the cell. "Get me a stool, and a new candle."

The guard closed the door again before walking down the passage to retrieve them. He came back with a short wooden stool and two candleholders, with half-used sticks. "I'm sorry this is all I could find on short notice." He opened the cell door once more, and placed the stool gingerly next to Jonah, his large hands dwarfing the wooden candleholders he placed atop the seat. He stepped out quickly, locking the cell door behind him.

Will sat up, still in the darkness. He watched, saying nothing while Jonah lit the two candles with his lantern. He placed the candles in front of Will's mat, lighting up his face.

Jonah had broad cheekbones, with his face thinner towards a delicate chin. His shoulders was slightly rounded, but his posture remained upright. Even in the dull light of his cell, Will could make out faint small pox marks on his cheeks, made all the more stark on his pale face.

Jonah sat on the stool and waited for Will to speak. Will held his glance and said nothing. The Reverend drew in a deep breath through his nostrils and exhaled slowly. He nodded his head to the neat pile of clothing by Will's mat.

"I see you gots a new frock coat and a pair of pumps for your big day. The guard tells me you turned down the offer to hire mourners," said Jonah. "'Tis a shame if your new finery will be blackened by boiling copper pitch, swinging from a gibbet."

"As opposed to being soiled by farkin' grubs and shite in a coffin?" Will said. "I'll go as I please."

"You have no authority as to the resting place of your corpse. Do you think our Lord cares about what clothes you wear on the day you meet him?"

"You want to discuss silks?" Will asked quietly.

"I'm here to discuss the matter of your soul."

"On whose authority?" said Will.

"I am trying to help you," said Jonah, ignoring his question. "Repent, so that God may have mercy on your soul."

"You keep gammon on to make amends for hangin' me," said Will.

"Forgiveness is unlikely, when one shows no remorse," said Jonah.

"Remorse for what? Fightin' for the right for men to feed their families?"

"Aigh. I'm well-versed in the Chartist hymns. You might fool your listeners under the sun, but God sees your heart."

"Yer would do well to remember that Chaplain."

"You are no benefactor nor victim. Like your friend, Cuffay. A convicted felon. A rootless, gutless vagabond. A stain that will soon be obliterated from this earth for your crimes and yet, still you persist with your fiction. I fear for you a great reckoning unless you repent, boy" Jonah persisted.

"You preach law, not gospel," said Will.

"So you know gospel, but understand it not?"

"Yer nouse nothin' of me, yet yer talk as if yer understand me," Will retorted.

Jonah paused. "Perhaps you are right. I shall delay my judgement until I have heard your full story then."

Will sat in silence.

"Well carry on. I am waiting."

"I'm goin' to sleep."

"You will have time to sleep, soon enough." Jonah leaned forward.

Will sighed. Looking at his hands, he spoke softly. "What I see is that the whole press and middle classes of this country raised a prejudice against the workin' poor and immigrants. We is taunted by the press, and smothered in ridicule, and youse has don' everythin' to crush the workin' poor and the alien. I ask for neither pity nor mercy - from man. I did not expect anythin' other than the verdict of guilty, right or wrong. I know the cause is good, and I have a self-approvin' conscience that will bear me up against yer slander, and that would bear me up even to the scaffold; there I know I will endure me punishment with pride. Yer do me nay disgrace by callin' me a felon. Nay. Yer honour me," said Will harshly, in tears.

"You are condemned, boy," said Jonah.

"When I shall find a time, I will judge uprightly," whispered Will as he turned away and faced the wall.

* * *

"Pop yer peepers Will. Yer have a visitor," said the Turnkey, as he opened Will's cell door.

Will opened his eyes and blinked. It was morning. He didn't want Jonah to be the last face he saw before he died. So he kept his back to the door, pretending to sleep.

An arm touched his shoulder. "Gethyn."

Startled, Will turned around and saw Lovett smiling down at him. "Lovett!" He cried and grabbed hold of Lovett's shirt, pulling him down, and there they laid, crying and hugging for a few minutes, before Lovett pulled him gently up.

Will wiped his tears on his filthy sleeve. "I didn't nay what's happened

"What's the point? Today I'm to be hanged."

to everyone? We've all been kept separate. What of Jacob?"

Lovett cleared his throat and held Will's arm. "Jacob's dead. Walter White and Dr Berry are runnin' the coffeehouse now. Would yer believe it? They're actually gettin' along," said Lovett.

Will wept.

Lovett waited a few minutes before he spoke again.

"I have some news for yer. Will?" Lovett squeezed Will's arm gently.

Will looked up. "What's the point. Today I'm to be hanged," cried Will. "I loved a gal, but I... I never got to hold her," sobbed Will.

Lovett choked. "Yer not meetin' yer Maker today son. That's why I'm here. Turns out yer old friend still has a few sympathetic squirrels at parliament. I've negotiated a royal pardon for yer. And Cuffay and High Toby too. Youse all bein' transported for life to different colonies in Australia. Cuffay and Toby are goin' to Van Dieman's Land. Youse bein' marked to a colony in New South Wales. Yer ship's at the Royal Docklands. It leaves tomorra, and Cuffay and Toby are leavin' in a few months' time," said Lovett.

"What of O'Connor?" asked Will in disbelief.

"He's okay. He was nay arrested. Some are sayin' he's goin' mad. We may have had our disagreements, but, I nouse the man. He's not mad. He just got...he just...his heart broke. Some men get over it. Other's never recover. I guess time will tell," said Lovett.

Lovett sighed. "Listen to me Gethyn. Hear me well. I have to go in a few minutes and I'll never see yer again. But I wanted to tell yer, that youse is a brave, upright lad. And yer Da would have been proud of yer. Transportation... I'll tell it to yer square, it's goin' to be hard. It's a long, cruel journey. They'll chain yer up in a rottin' hulk for eight months. There may be up ter fifty convicts in one cell, that is divided into tiny compartments by wooden and iron bars. One in ten prisoners survive the voyage. I want yer to prepare yer heart for the travail. Yer young, and yer brave. And God Almighty has preserved yer life to do great things. I believe it in me heart. Nay, I don't just believe it, Gethyn, I nouse it. So take courage, young Gethyn, and nay give up. Yer will survive this, and yer will go on and carry the legacy of the chartists to the other side of the world. Learn from the mistake made by O'Connor. Listen to me young Gethyn. Unsustained head-on mass rallies are just populist trite. See how the march was over before it began? All dat work, for nothin! Yer must learn the system, and implode it from within," said Lovett.

"Time's up," the Turnkey rattled the bar with a sharp knock of his baton.

"Did yer hear me Gethyn?" asked Lovett urgently. "It's not the show. It's knowin' the system," implored Lovett.

"Aight. I hears' yer. Youse got to be a nousy farka," said Gethyn.

Lovett laughed with relief. "That's me boy. Safe travels and God be wid yer, yer nousy farka".

- The End of Part One -

References

Abrahamic Scriptures

Anglicus, Ducange (1859). The Vulgar Tongue: A Glossary of Slang, Cant and Flash Words and Phrases used in London 1839-1859. Second Edition, Bernard Quaritch, London.

Anon, (1845). The National Chartist Hymn Book. National Chartists Association, Rochdale: North Britain.

Anon. Dens of London Exposed. Undated. Forgotten Books.

Ashton, Rosemary (2012). Victorian Bloomsbury. Yale University Press, New Haven, USA.

Benson, John (1980). British Coal-Miners in the Nineteenth Century: A Social History. Holmes & Meier.

Berger, Stefan Llafur (2001). 'Working-Class Culture and the Labour Movement in the South Wales and the Ruhr Coalfields, 1850-2000: A Comparison'. Journal of Welsh Labour History/Cylchgrawn Hanes Llafur Cymru (8) (2) pp 5-40.

Brodie, Marc (2003). 'Free Trade and Cheap Theatre: Sources of Politics for the Nineteenth-Century London Poor'. Social History. (Vol. 28) No. 3, Taylor & Francis Ltd

Chase, Malcolm (2007). 'Chartism's Black Activist', British Humanities Index, (Vol. 57) No.10.

Chase, Malcolm (2009). 'Labour's Candidates': Chartist Challenges at the Parliamentary Polls 1839–1860'. Labour History Review, (Vol. 74) No.1, University of Leeds, UK pp 64–89.

Curtis, Ben (2011). 'A Tradition of Radicalism: The Politics of the South Wales Miners, 1964-1985', Labour History Review (Vol, 76) No.1 pp 34-50.

Goodway, David (1982). London Chartism 1838-1848. Cambridge University Press, Cambridge UK.

Jankiewicz, Stephen (2012). 'A Dangerous Class: The Street Sellers of Nineteenth-Century London'. Journal of Social History. (Vol. 46), No. 2, Oxford University Press, pp. 391-415.

Sheppard, Francis (1998). London: A History. Oxford University Press, New York.

Vaux, James Hardy (1812). A New and Comprehensive Vocabulary of the Flash Language. Dodo Press

ACKNOWLEDGMENTS

Many thanks to the following people who kindly donated their time and smarts to make this book possible:

Brendan Smith

Brendon Clements, Bloomfield Colliery Ashtonfield,
Bloomfield Group NSW

Frederick Smith

Grant Sullivan, Clarence Colliery, Centennial Coal NSW

My darling family, Joseph, Bethany and Valerie Smith

Joanne Leila Smith

About the Author

With a career as a communications professional for the past 17 years, Joanne Leila Smith is currently the Managing Editor of INDVSTRVS, and international business publication based in Sydney, Australia. This book is Joanne's first foray into historical-fiction, and is her fourth book published. Joanne is a professional member with the Australian Institute of Professional Editors (iPed), The Australian Society of Authors (ASA) and NSW Institute of Teachers (BOSTES). Her qualifications include: Master of Arts (English), Bachelor of Arts (Media & Communications), Diploma of Journalism, and Graduate Diploma of Education (Double-method English). Joanne lives on the Central Coast NSW with her best friend and husband, Joseph, and their two sweet daughters.

About the Artist

Darlene Lavett is an emerging Australian Artist, whom has been painting from a young age. After graduating in Commercial Art at Queensland College of Art, Darlene had a successful career as a Captain in the Australian Army and in Advertising. Showcasing her photorealistic style in her 'Modern Reflections' solo exhibition (2016) Darlene's work is starting to receive national recognition and an international following. Since picking up the brush again two years ago, Darlene became a finalist for three recent national art prizes including the National Kennedy Art Prize, National Cambridge Studio Gallery Prize and Gallipoli Art Prize. Darlene lives in Brisbane Qld with her husband, a Jack Russell, Toy Poodle and Bengal Cat. www.darlenelavettartist.com

Cover Design and Layout

Briar Forrester Graphic Design. www.briarforrester.com.

www.ingramcontent.com/pod-product-compliance
Lightning Source LLC
Chambersburg PA
CBHW052143220626
47052CB00005B/1172